For Shane and Jenna

Text and illustrations copyright © 2003 by Jim Arnosky
All rights reserved. This book, or parts thereof, may not be reproduced in any form without permission
in writing from the publisher, G. P. Putnam's Sons, a division of Penguin Putnam Books for Young Readers,
345 Hudson Street, New York, NY 10014. G. P. Putnam's Sons, Reg. U.S. Pat. & Tm. Off.
Published simultaneously in Canada. Manufactured in China by South China Printing Co. (1988) Ltd.
Designed by Gunta Alexander. Text set in Stempel Schneidler.
The art was done in watercolor.
Library of Congress Cataloging-in-Publication Data
Arnosky, Jim. Armadillo's orange / Jim Arnosky.
p. cm.   Summary: An armadillo remembers where his burrow is by the orange near the opening,
but when the orange rolls away, he discovers a new way to find his home.
1. Armadillos—Juvenile fiction. [1. Armadillos—Fiction. 2. Animals—Fiction.] I. Title.
PZ10.3.A86923 Ar 2003   [E]—dc21   2002006356   ISBN 0-399-23412-8
5 7 9 10 8 6 4
First Impression

JIM ARNOSKY

Armadillo's Orange

G. P. PUTNAM'S SONS • NEW YORK

At the wild edge of an orange grove,

a young armadillo dug a burrow in soft, sandy soil.

Close by lay a big, round orange that had fallen

from its tree. The orange made it easy for

Armadillo to find his brand-new home.

Each day Armadillo left his burrow

to hunt for insects and grubs to eat.

He followed a narrow path

that wound its way

around the tangled stems

of plants and trees.

Every time he walked the winding path,

Armadillo passed beneath a lively green snake

climbing on a branch.

But Armadillo never looked up.

He just hurried on his way.

Down the path, a shy rattlesnake was coiled
in the shade of big, drooping leaves.
But Armadillo quickly waddled by,
looking only straight ahead.

Then an old, slow-moving tortoise
crossed the path.
Armadillo had to stop and wait.
He shuffled his feet impatiently
until the tortoise passed.

He hurried onto a fallen tree where he could dig in the rotting wood for tasty grubs.

A scrub jay called out in its loud, raspy voice. Armadillo closed his ears. Honeybees buzzed by on their way to their hive.

Armadillo covered his face with his long claws.

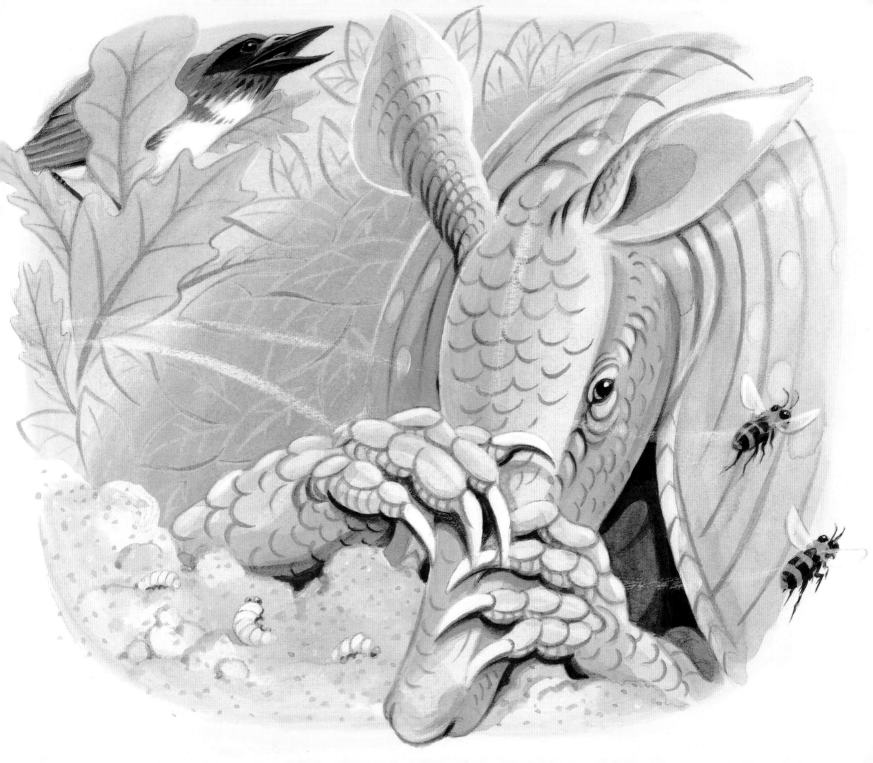

When the other animals had finally gone,

Armadillo gobbled up every grub

that he could find. Then he rushed back

down the path. When he saw the big, round orange,

he knew that he was home.

Every day was the same.

But one day, while Armadillo was away,

a sudden gust of wind blew through the grove.

The wind pushed Armadillo's orange

just enough to make it roll downhill into a weedy ditch.

When Armadillo returned, he could not find his burrow.

He walked and walked, looking for the orange

that marked the entrance to his home.

Everything seemed strange and wrong

with the big, round orange gone.

Armadillo wandered, lost and all alone.

Then, suddenly, he smelled the sweet scent of honeybees

and saw the old tortoise slowly crossing the path.

Together, Armadillo and Tortoise

watched the honeybees buzz by.

Then Armadillo heard the scrub jay calling in its raspy voice. He followed the sound, and soon he came upon the shy rattlesnake resting in the shade. When Armadillo looked up, he saw the lively green snake climbing on a branch.

Armadillo smelled and heard and saw these things and knew that he was home.

Armadillo missed the big, round orange
shining brightly near his hole.
But with neighbors living all around,
he didn't need it anymore.

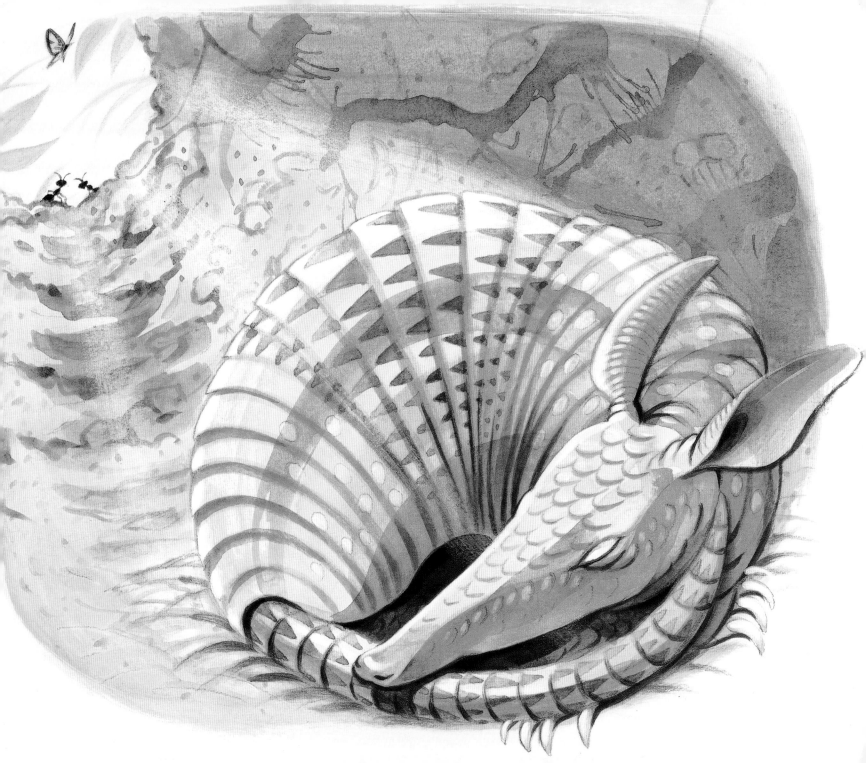